A 2ND LEVEL ADVENTURE SET IN THE DARK TOWER CAMPAIGN SETTING

Writer: Stephen Newton • Cover artist: Aaron Kreader • Editor: Brian Gilkison
Cartographer: Will McAusland • Interior Artists: Joe Abboreno, Alex Coggon, Tom Galambos, Doug Kovacs, Cliff Kurowski, Brad McDevitt, Chad Sergesketter, Matt Sutton, and Del Tiegler • Art direction & layout: Matt Hildebrand
Developer: Michael Curtis • Dark Tower Master: Joseph Goodman

IN MEMORY OF JENNELL JAQUAYS (1956-2024).

T0284018

BY MITRA'S BONES, MEET THY DOOM!

INTRODUCTION

y *Mitra's Bones, Meet Thy Doom!* is a Dungeon Crawl Classics RPG adventure designed for four to five 2nd-level characters. It can be played as a standalone adventure or as a prequel to *Dark Tower*. *Dark Tower* is not a requirement to play this adventure, but judges will find that being familiar with the locations and NPCs of *Dark Tower* is useful. As a prequel, it provides story hooks for PCs to visit Mitra's Fist and backstories for the NPCs in that adventure without giving away too many spoilers. In most playtests, it took two sessions to complete the adventure.

ADVENTURE BACKGROUND

THE BIRTH OF GODS

sk any bard from Xa Deshret and they will tell you the most popular ballad they're requested to perform is *The Rise of the White Tower*, a tale recounting Mitra's mutual fight to the death with the demon Set. While seemingly a heroic tale of Mitra's conquest over evil, the poem overlooks the ugly consequences of Set's defeat whispered by theologians in dusty libraries: by destroying Set's material demon form, Mitra allowed Set to rise as a *god* of Chaos!

The followers of Mitra concluded that the way to counter Set's rising influence was to deify Mitra so he too could continue his crusade as a god himself! Mitra's body was exhumed and his bones distributed between his loyal followers—now fledgling apostles. Their mission: use the holy relics of Mitra's bones to attract new followers to newly constructed shrines dedicated in his name. One of the most popular sites was the renowned White Tower of Mitra built atop Mitra's original sanctuary in the town of Mitra's Fist. But there were also less grand temples, such as the one built near the tiny waystation of Mitra's Cross. Nonetheless, the shrine in Mitra's Cross became a pilgrimage site for the pious eager to see a fragment of Mitra's mortal self: his actual teeth harvested from his corpse after his death, and the Weeping Maiden, a statue rumored to bestow miracles on those who believe!

OPPOSING TEMPLES

ut even gods submit to astral laws of symmetry that mankind observes but will never understand. Wherever Mitra's devotees established a presence, Set—now a god—was compelled to answer in kind. Near these sites, Set sent his own followers to antagonize the Mitraic priests and prevent their nascent religion from thriving. When the temple of Mitra's Cross was consecrated with the Mitraic relic, Set demanded that an opposing temple of equal size and power be erected. In his dark temple, Set placed a relic of his own: a fang from his slain demon form. As the temple was considered modest (by Set's standards), Set did not send any entity nearly as powerful as one of his Chosen Sons, but instead sent Mahna, one of his numerous runt offspring, to watch over the artifact.

> "WARE YE PILGRIM! YE HAVE BEEN TOUCHED BY THE HAND OF MITRA. CAUSE NO EVIL IN THIS, HIS SHRINE, ELSE YE SHALL DIE MOST HORRIBLY."
>
> — *Dark Tower*, Jennell Jaquays

THE ARRIVAL OF AVVANI AND AKKE[N]

pproximately 300 years ago, clerics of Set—Avva[ni] and her brother Akken—departed their home [in] Mitra's Fist, leaving their spouses and childr[en] behind to attend to Set's temple. The siblings believed th[ey] would be rewarded with "eternal life" for their efforts. S[et] delivered on that promise… in his own way. Avvani a[nd] Akken were freed from time's ravages upon the flesh, wi[th] one condition: they were forbidden to travel more than fi[ve] miles from the temple's unholy relic, the *Fang of Set*, le[st] their age come due. Mahna has been forbidden from allo[w]ing others to come in possession of the *Fang*, including f[ol]lowers of Set. Thus, Avvani and Akken have been trapp[ed] in the tiny village of Mitra's Cross for the last three cen[tu]ries—bitter allies, neighbors, and sometimes lovers—lo[ok]ing for a loophole which will allow them to one day retu[rn] home to the families they left behind.

As the decades crawled by, Avvani and Akken becam[e] increasingly resentful, watching as Mitraic pilgrims we[re] drawn to the temple and its legends of the miracles p[er]formed by the Weeping Maiden. Knowing they lacked t[he] power to defeat the temple's guardians, they did the ne[xt] best thing: they bribed a local stone giant, Gabbro, to c[on]ceal both temples, burying both of them under a great cai[rn] of rocks. Once concealed, the couple, along with their s[on] Dakkar, created a "false shrine of Mitra" upon the site of t[he] original, robbing and killing gullible Mitraic faithful who [ar]rived seeking out miracles.

And now, when strangers arrive in town, Avvani and A[k]ken evaluate whether the newcomers should be consider[ed] fodder to be exploited, or marks that could help them rec[ov]er the *Fang of Set* so that they might escape their immortal [im]clause.

RUNNING THE ADVENTURE

NPCs: Most NPC hold knowledge and/or rumors about t[he] adventure's plot which can be gleaned through interacti[ng] with the NPC via role play. An NPC's knowledge and [mo]tives are written in their bios (see Appendix A: Drama[tis] Personae).

There is a complex, co-dependent relationship between t[he] NPCs of this adventure. If Avvani or Akken is attacked, t[he] other immediately knows and sprints to the aid of the oth[er] within 1d3 rounds, bringing their NPC companions (Jicc [and] Rah) to assist. If Jicc is attacked and escapes, the entire fa[m]ily attempts to hunt down the PCs.

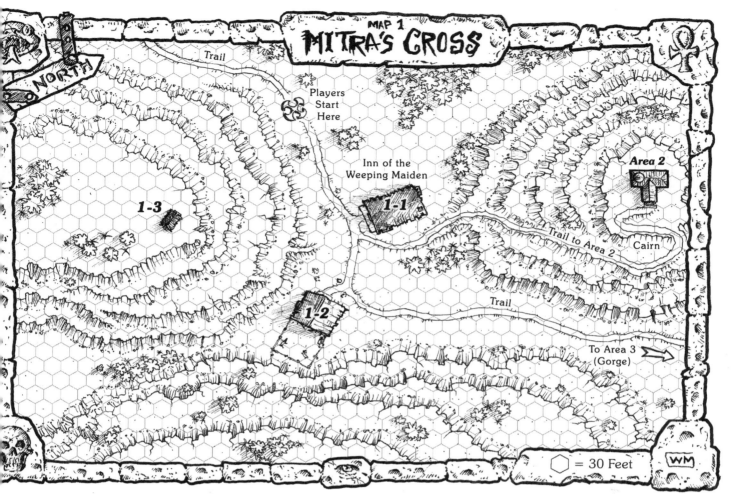

ADVENTURE HOOKS

The PCs begin the adventure arriving in the remote town of Mitra's Cross, renowned for being the closest settlement to the Mitraic temple containing the miracle-performing Weeping Maiden and not much else. The following are a few adventure hooks the judge can leverage:

The PCs have heard rumors of the Mitraic shrine containing the Weeping Maiden, a divine statue which legend says can perform miracles to Mitra's faithful, and have travelled from afar to pay their respects.

As penance to remove deity disapproval, a cleric in the party has been asked to locate missing Acolytes Rupert and Chilton, two clerics of Mitra who have not been heard from in several months.

A spellcaster's patron has conveyed that the tiny hamlet of Mitra's Cross is not as quiet as it seems, and that nefarious forces are working to keep magic items the patron wishes to acquire for themselves hidden from prying eyes.

AREA 1: MITRA'S CROSS

e Map 1: Mitra's Cross

rched and covered in dust, your party has arrived at the tiny ystation of Mitra's Cross, nestled in the foothills of the Moun-

tains of the Fifth Prince. The hamlet is little more than a dirt-packed road surrounded by a few weather-beaten structures.

To the southeast is a small mud-brick building adorned with a sign which reads, "The Inn of the Weeping Maiden." From an open window, an elderly woman watches your approach.

Further down the path is another slightly larger structure with an attached animal pen currently housing four camels. The animals look lethargic and slightly underfed.

Between the two buildings, a stone marker points up a trail leading into the rocky hills. Another smaller path winds around the base of the hill to the southeast.

If the PCs reconnoiter the area, they also discover a smaller path leading to area 1-3.

Area 1-1 – Inn of the Weeping Maiden: The inn (see Map 1a: The Inn of the Weeping Maiden) is a two-story mud-brick structure with an open landing on the second floor. It has no glass windows, but open ports in the walls provide ventilation and light (and are large enough for a thief to crawl through). PCs attempting to climb to the 2nd story landing or roof must make a DC 10 *climb sheer surfaces* check or fall for 1d6 damage.

Area 1-1A – Main Room: *The main room of the inn consists of a serving area with four tables and an unlit fireplace. A set of stairs leads up to the guest rooms, and a rear door leads into what appears to be the kitchen.*

At the table nearest the fireplace, a middle-aged man is slumped over and sleeping, a half-consumed tankard of warm beer on the table in front of him. The man's lips and skin have taken on an unhealthy gray pallor.

At a corner table, two dwarves are drinking and quietly chatting to each other in Dwarvish.

Near the rear door stands a lean young man wearing a simple cotton kilt. He has the dull-eyed look of a simpleton.

Finally, a toothless, elderly woman, with skin so thin and dry it appears translucent, greets you. She wears a simple cotton dress and a bracelet with gleaming gems. Her chapped lips crack open into a smile as she says, "Welcome, pilgrims, to the Weeping Maiden! What can I offer you to slake your thirst?"

Avvani (aka "Vani"): As the characters parley, the old woman (she could easily pass for 90) introduces herself as "Vani." She is friendly and offers the PCs wine and camel stew, ordering Jicc into the kitchen to prepare whatever the party requests. Vani gladly makes small talk and assumes the PCs are heading to the shrine. Indeed, she acts surprised if the PCs say they are in town for any other purpose ("Why would you travel all the way to Mitra's Cross and not see the famous shrine?"). She offers the PCs room and board at inflated prices (15 sp per night). If asked, she will mention that she came to Mitra's Cross many years ago on a trip with her brother who passed away long ago. She would love to go home again someday to the town of Mitra's Fist and visit her late husband's family, but the journey would be too perilous at her age. She hopes that one day the Weeping Maiden in the "shrine on the rocky hill" will give her a sign of how she could safely make the journey back.

Avvani wears a fine silver bracelet housing five gems, each worth 10 gp and etched with a unique hieroglyph symbol; two of the gems are encased in an ankh. If asked, she explains the gems represent her five children, and the two encased in the ankh represent "her two which have passed to dust." Concealed in her dress she wears *Set's Dagger of the Gazing Cobra* (see Appendix B: New Magic Items) and carries the key which opens her bedroom door (area 1-1E) and the wardrobe within.

Avvani (priestess of Set): Init +0; Atk dagger +2 melee (1d4+1 plus hypnosis [see *Set's Dagger of the Gazing Cobra*]); Crit III/d10; AC 12; HD 4d8 (hp 22); MV 30'; Act 1d20; SP cleric abilities ((+6 spell check): divine aid, lay on hands, turn unholy), immune to poison, spellcasting (+6 spell check): Spells (1st) *animal summoning (snakes), food of the gods, holy sanctuary, paralysis, second sight, word of command*; (2nd) *divine symbol, lotus stare, neutralize poison or disease, snake charm*; SV Fort +2, Ref +1, Will +4; AL C.

Jicc: Jicc has worked many years for Avvani and is loyal to her out of fear. His prolonged subjugation to her spellcasting has left him mentally diminished. Vani avoids leaving Jicc unattended with the PCs for any extended length of time. If the PCs attempt to question him, she gives him a harsh slap and commands him, "BACK TO THE KITCHEN!" If the PCs manage to isolate Jicc from Vani without the threat of violence, he provides his NPC knowledge.

Jicc (laborer): Init +1; Atk punch +1 melee (1d3, subdual); Crit III/d6; AC 10; HD 1d4 (hp 4); MV 30'; Act 1d20; SV Fo[rt] -2, Ref -2, Will +2; AL N.

Acolyte Bentley: The man "sleeping" at the corner table [is] Acolyte Bentley. He is not inebriated but drugged with de[s]ert salamander venom (see area 2-0) which Avvani slips in[to] his drink each night (this is also the cause of his lips appe[ar]ing gray). Avvani keeps Bentley in a stupor as occasional[ly] the Mitraic church sends emissaries to check on him, an[d] she doesn't want to risk anything that might disrupt he[r] operation. Bentley can be awakened for 1d3 rounds with [a] successful 2 dice *lay on hands*, a successful *neutralize poison [or] disease* spell, or if the PCs can manage to prevent Avvani an[d] Jicc from drugging him for 24 hours. Once revived, Bentle[y] provides all the rumors and lore he knows. The stats belo[w] represent a fully revived Bentley; while drugged, he has th[e] stats of a peasant (see DCC RPG p. 434).

Acolyte Bentley (1st level cleric): Init +0; Atk punch +0 m[e]lee (1d3, subdual); Crit III/d8; AC 11; HD 1d8+1 (hp 9); M[V] 30'; Act 1d20; SP cleric abilities ((+2 spell check): divine a[id], lay on hands, turn unholy), spellcasting (+2 spell chec[k]: Spells (1st) *detect evil, detect magic, invisible to unholy* (see A[p]pendix C: New Spells), *protection from evil*; SV Fort +2, Ref [+2], Will +2; AL L.

Shton & Shlex: The two dwarves, Shton and Shlex, are tw[o] brothers who arrived in town three days ago. If approache[d] they are friendly, happy to make conversation with the p[ar]ty, and even offer to buy them a round of drinks. They sa[y] they have no intention of visiting the temple as their bu[si]ness is to the east in Redmoon Pass. However, if the PC[s] are stealthy and eavesdrop (and can understand Dwarvis[h]) they learn the two are there to investigate the "stone gia[nt] on the other side of the mountain" and see if they can ste[al] the wealth he has no doubt accumulated!

Shton/Shlex (dwarven adventurers): Init +1; Atk battlea[xe] or warhammer +3 melee (1d8+2); Crit III/d8; AC 14; H[D] 2d12 (hp 26 each); MV 20'; Act 1d20; SP dwarf abilities ([in]fravision 60', smell gems, find construction); SV Fort +2, R[ef] +0, Will +2; AL N.

Area 1-1B – Kitchen: The kitchen contains shelves [of] meal ingredients (camel jerky, spices, bread), serving plat[es] and drinking cups. A small table holds pots and cooki[ng] utensils and a stove is built into the east wall. A stairca[se] leads down to area 1-1G.

Concealed behind a haunch of camel jerky is the key whi[ch] unlocks the door to Bentley's room (area 1-1D).

Area 1-1C – Empty Guest Room: This unoccupi[ed] guest room contains a floor mat of woven straw, a small [ta]ble with a water basin, a bedpan, and a wooden bed cover[ed] with a camel hide blanket. In the empty northwestern gue[st] room, a prayer book of Mitra has been mislaid and forg[ot]ten under the table. On the inner cover is inscribed the na[me] "Acolyte Rupert."

Area 1-1D – Bentley's Room: The door to this room [is] locked (DC 12 *pick lock*); the key is kept in area 1-1B. T[he]

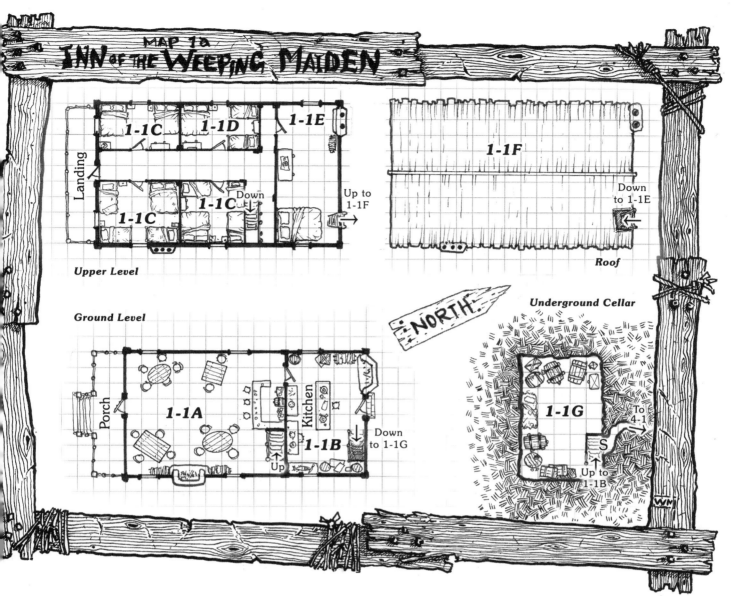

Upper Level

1-1C 1-1D 1-1E

1-1C

Landing

1-1C

Down

Up to 1-1F

1-1F

Down to 1-1E

Roof

Ground Level

NORTH

Underground Cellar

Porch

1-1A

Kitchen

1-1B

Up

Down to 1-1G

1-1G

To 4-1

S

Up to 1-1B

...om is furnished similar to the other guest rooms (area 1C). Unlike those rooms, there is a faint scent of pepper in ...e air (from the desert salamander venom).

...n the table is an ivory carving of a lion (a Mitraic holy ...mbol), as well as a small prayer book which can be used ...a scroll containing the spells *blessing* and *holy sanctuary* ...he reader makes the spell check). Inscribed on the inside ...ver is the message, "Acolyte Bentley, may Mitra provide ...u with a lion's courage and freedom from temptation of ...n and impurity as you make your pilgrimage to visit the ...essed Maiden. Yours in strength, Curate Glossop."

...ch night, Jicc carries a seemingly intoxicated Acolyte Bent-...y into this room after Avvani gives him a final "nightcap."

...rea 1-1E – Avvani's Personal Chamber: The door to ...is room is locked (DC 12 *pick lock*); Avvani keeps the key ...her pocket. This bedroom is twice as wide as the guest ...ooms and contains a couch; a table with a mirror, perfumes, ...d cosmetics; and a closed and locked wardrobe closet. On ...small pedestal near the window are five jade figurines. A ...all ladder leads through an opening in the ceiling and ...ovides access to the roof.

Jade Figurines: The jade figurines are carved animals (an owl, cat, viper, beetle, and ibis) and are worth 25 gp each. Two of the figurines (the owl and ibis) have a small silver ankh on a chain looped over them. The figurines are representations of Avvani's five children, including the two who have died (Avvaar and Akkar).

Wardrobe: The wardrobe is locked (DC 12 *pick lock*). Concealed behind Avvani's clothes on the back wall of the wardrobe is a portrait of a portly looking merchant and beautiful young woman in formal wedding attire. Lurking behind the couple is a grotesque four-armed man with the body of snake. The portrait says, "The wedding of Avvakris & Avvani under the fangs of Set and His Chosen Son Manahath." There is an artist's signature ("Haffrung H.") and it is dated approximately 325 years prior.

In addition to containing her clothes, the wardrobe is also the lair of Avvani's pet cobra, Slithis, who has a 60% chance of a surprise attack when the wardrobe door is opened.

Slithis (large cobra): Init +0 (surprise); Atk bite +3 melee (1d3 plus poison [+1d3 damage, DC 13 Fort negates]); Crit M/d6; AC 11; HD 1d4 (hp 2); MV 30', climb 15'; Act 1d20; SP surprises 60% of time; SV Fort +1, Ref +1, Will +0; AL N.

Area 1-1F – Roof: *From the roof of the inn, you have a scenic view of the entire town, including the camel pen and the temple at the top of a rocky hill to the east. From this vantage point, you can also see something you hadn't noticed before—a small cabin nestled beneath some trees on the hillside to the west.*

On the roof itself there is a simple bed of dried leaves and camel hides. Next to the bed is a T-shaped wooden pedestal.

The hillside cabin is area 1-3.

Avvani sleeps on the roof at night where it is much cooler and she can keep an eye on her surroundings. She can be found here between midnight and sunrise with Nek, her pet vulture. Nek hunts during the day, but if PCs are present during daylight hours, there is a 1-in-4 chance that Nek will notice and attack the party.

Nek (large vulture): Init +1; Atk peck +2 melee (1d3); Crit M/d4; AC 13; HD 1d3 (hp 2); MV 5', fly 35'; SP infravision 60'; Act 1d20; SV Fort +1, Ref +1, Will +0; AL N.

Area 1-1G – Cellar: *This cellar is stocked with several barrels and various packages of dried goods. A man snores loudly on a cot in the corner.*

In this cool cellar are several barrels of beer, as well as 16 bottles of wine bearing the "Weeping Maiden" label. Concealed behind the bottles (easily found if PCs search) is a small flask containing a yellow liquid which smells like pepper. The liquid is desert salamander venom which Avvani slips into Acolyte Bentley's beer each night.

Desert salamander venom: Delivery: ingestion; DC 12 Fortitude; Damage on successful save: -2 to attack rolls and lethargy; Damage on failed saved: sleep for 3d4 hours; Recovery: normal healing.

Secret door: Under the stairs on the east wall is a secret door (DC 12 Intelligence check to locate). Once opened, it reveals a tunnel leading to area 4-1.

Kimmer: Passed out on the cot in the cellar is Kimmer, an overweight human male in his 60s. If awakened, Kimmer reveals he arrived in town 3 months ago. Initially, he didn't intend to stay, but Avvani has been very kind to him and provides him room and shelter in the cellar as long as he occasionally performs favors for her. He mentions that he frequently sees Jicc sneaking into the wine, which he finds odd, as he doesn't think Jicc drinks. While not brave, he will come to Avvani's aid if she is threatened.

Kimmer: Init -1; Atk dagger +0 melee (1d4); Crit III/d4; AC 10; HD 1d6 (hp 3); MV 30'; Act 1d20; SV Fort -1, Ref -1, Will +0; AL C.

Area 1-2 – Camel Traders: *A strapping human male merchant approximately thirty years old nods as your approach. The man wears a kilt and is shirtless, exposing several animal tattoos inked onto his chest. He also wears an extraordinary set of boots whose tips are taxidermied cobras positioned as if ready to strike! Standing beneath a canopy, the man haggles with a middle-aged human woman over the goods he has for sale: grapes, figs, pomegranates, camel sausage, and various trinkets. From somewhere behind his small store, you hear the pitiful bleat of camels.*

Akken (aka "Ken"): Akken introduces himself as "Ken" [to] the PCs. He has two distinctive tattoos on his chest: a beet[le] and an ibis, both surrounded by ankhs. If asked about h[is] extravagant boots, he answers they were fashioned out [of] two cobras he slew with his bare hands.

Akken's goods have a 30% markup over prices found i[n] the DCC RPG rulebook. Camels can be purchased for 90 g[p] each or rented for 2 gp per week with a 75 gp deposit.

Akken wears a shendyt (a loincloth similar to a kilt) an[d] *Set's Boots of the Spitting Cobra* (see Appendix B), and has [a] dagger strapped to his waist at all times.

Akken (Priest of Set): Init +0; Atk dagger +3 melee (1d4+2); Crit III/d10; AC 12; HD 4d8+1 (hp 24); MV 30'; Act 1d2[0]; SP cleric abilities ((+4 spell check): divine aid, lay on hand[s], turn unholy), immune to poison, spellcasting (+4 spe[ll] check): Spells (1st) *animal summoning (snakes), darkness, dete[ct] magic, holy sanctuary, protection from evil, word of comman[d]* (2nd): *cure paralysis, curse, snake charm, stinging stone*; SV Fo[rt] +2, Ref -1, Will +4; AL C.

Ramaya: The haggling woman is Ramaya, an uncurse[d] loner who lives in the hills and who visits the town once [a] month for supplies. She mostly keeps to herself, but if tre[at]ed kindly, she advises the PCs that they would be best [to] finish their business in Mitra's Cross as quickly as possib[le] and move on. She also advises to stick to the main road t[he] way they came and avoid the shortcut, as there is a cave be[ast] that lives in that area.

Inside the mud-brick building are Akken and Rahkert's li[v]ing quarters. Hidden under a stone beneath their bed is [a] *potion of human control* (which is also effective against gian[ts], see DCC RPG p. 224) and a 12" tall black tourmaline statu[e] of a human body with the head of a jackal (Set). The stat[u]ette is a holy symbol to Set and has *Set's Prayer Against Mit[ra]* inscribed on the bottom: "Almighty Set, Father of the Fo[ur] Chosen Sons. You are the Lion's dread. May your veno[m] cleanse this and all worlds of its mongrels. Wherever th[e] cur rises, so shall your Sons." (The prayer is a clue for th[e] puzzle in area 6-1).

Akken's companion Rahkert (aka "Rah") is in the back ten[d]ing to the camels ("Sad Jim," "Beans," "Lord Snort," an[d] "Thin Rizzo"). Vijah is also in the back mending the cam[el] fence. Both Rahkert and Vijah will immediately come to A[k]ken's aid if the PCs act belligerently.

Rahkert: Init +2; Atk scimitar +2 melee (1d6+1); Crit 19-[20] III/d10; AC 12; HD 3d10+1 (hp 29); MV 30'; Act 1d20; S[V] Fort +2, Ref +1, Will +1; AL C.

Rahkert is a muscular man in his 20s. He wears a leath[er] smock (which provides a +1 bonus to AC), sandals, and ca[r]ries a hammer used for stable repairs.

Vijah: Init +2; Atk hammer +2 melee (1d6+1); Crit III/d[10]; AC 12; HD 2d8 (hp 14); MV 30'; Act 1d20; SV Fort +3, Re[f +1] Will +1; AL C.

Vijah is a wiry man in his mid-40s with leathery skin covered by cancerous blisters. He works for Akken during the day and squanders all his earnings on bad wine in the evenings.

Area 1-3 – Bentley's Abandoned Cabin: *This sparse cabin appears to have been deserted for at least several months. The only items of note are a few trinkets on a nightstand and a simple cot.*

PCs of lawful alignment can also see a small shelf in the corner of the cabin.

This was Acolyte Bentley's residence before he started being drugged by Avvani. The trinkets include his prayer chain adorned with small lions and swords, one of the many holy symbols of a Mitraic priest.

Shelf: A small corner shelf has been cloaked with an *invisible to unholy* spell, which is how it has gone undetected by the residents of Mitra's Cross. The items are visible to PCs of lawful alignments, or via a *detect invisible* spell. Cloaked by the spell is Bentley's prayer book and journal. Most of the journal is illegible due to Bentley's poor penmanship, but the following passages can be deciphered:

- First entry, dated two years ago: "Finally reached the foothills of the Mountains of the Fifth Prince! My year-long journey has been wearisome, but I must keep repeating the motto of Knight Graydon: The Righteous Journey is the Reward!"

- Second entry, dated eight months ago: "Arrived in Mitra's Cross. Vani and Ken have introduced themselves and have made me quite comfortable. They offered to escort me personally to the temple tomorrow so I may pay my respects to Our Holy Bicameral. No need, said I! I will make this last leg of the journey myself!"

- Third entry, same day as the second entry: "The serving boy mentioned a "Stone Man" living in the gorge before being pummeled into silence by Vani. Will investigate that after I pay my respects to Our Holy Bicameral."

- Final entry, dated one day after the third entry: "This simple wooden temple on the rocky hill is nothing like the glorious structure described to me by Curate Glossop! I dread the minions of the Most Sinful One have tainted this Holy Place with their foul wickedness. On the morrow I shall pray for Mitra's Righteousness and The Maiden's Divinity for guidance."

AREA 2: FALSE TEMPLE

See Map 2: False Temple

Area 2-0 – The Great Rock Cairn: *In a clearing between two rocky outcroppings rises a cairn of stones over three hundred feet high. Atop the great cairn is a modest structure resembling a simple church.*

Area 2-0 is at the base of the rock cairn.

Avvani and Akken negotiated with Gabbro to hide the original temple of Mitra under the stone cairn and replace it with a forgery of their own design. The couple designed the false

temple to lure gullible pilgrims in order to steal their offerings. Dwarves have a 1-in-4 chance of recognizing that the cairn does not appear natural.

Climbing the cairn to the false temple (area 2-1) is relatively easy, but on the ascent, the PCs are attacked by desert salamanders who make their lair in the rocks. Fighting on the cairn is hazardous and with each attack there is a 1-in-4 chance of falling (DC 12 Reflex save to avoid falling and starting their next round prone).

Desert salamander (3): Init -1; Atk bite +2 melee (1d4 plus lethargic poison); Crit M/d8; AC 13; HD 2d8+2 (hp 15, 15, 12); MV 30', climb 20'; Act 1d20; SP lethargic poison, eucalyptus anathema; SV Fort +1, Ref +2, Will -2; AL N.

Lethargic poison: When a desert salamander lands a successful bite attack, the opponent must make a DC 12 Fortitude save or suffer extreme lethargy, incurring a -2 penalty to all attack rolls for 1d3 rounds and reducing movement by half. The target's lips will also turn a shade of dull gray for 1d3 days.

Eucalyptus anathema: Desert salamanders find the smell of eucalyptus repellent, and will not attack PCs wearing eucalyptus oil or clothing made from eucalyptus leaves.

Desert salamanders are slender 3-foot-long reptiles and are natural predators to the area. They have a rubbery, sand-colored hide which secretes poison when close to prey. Their venom can be used to create desert salamander venom.

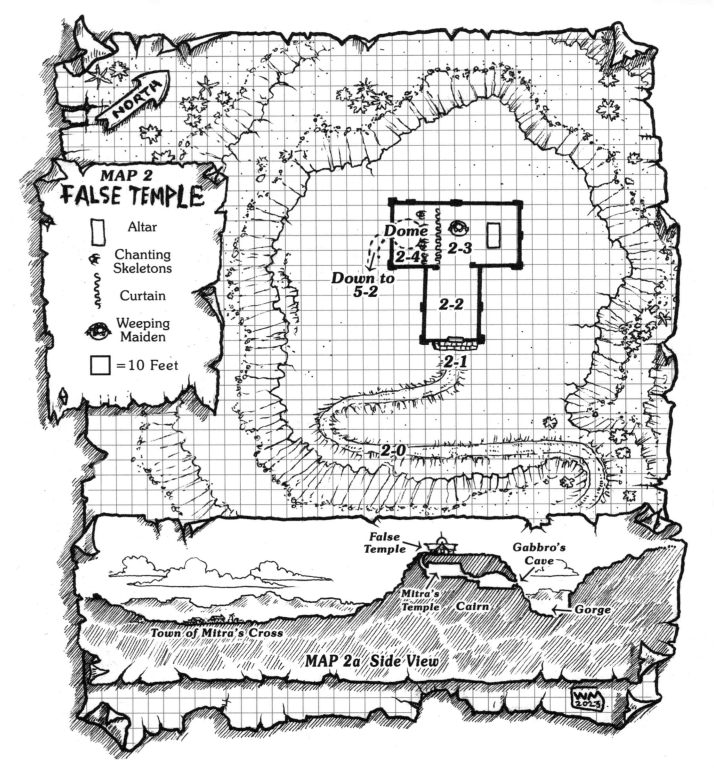

MAP 2
FALSE TEMPLE

▯ Altar

🐍 Chanting Skeletons

〰 Curtain

👁 Weeping Maiden

▯ = 10 Feet

NORTH

Dome
2-4

2-3

Down to 5-2

2-2

2-1

2-0

False Temple

Gabbro's Cave

Mitra's Temple

Cairn

Gorge

Town of Mitra's Cross

MAP 2a Side View

Area 2-1 – Outside Temple: *As you reach the crest of the hill, you finally lay eyes on the Temple of Mitra before you. The simple wooden structure has a single weather-beaten door and no windows. From this vantage point, you can see the inn far below, smoke slowly wafting up from its two chimneys.*

The smoke from the chimneys is Avvani's signal to Sword Dak to prepare for the PCs approaching the false temple.

Area 2-2 – Sword Dak: *The Temple of Mitra is much more modest than you expected, consisting of not much more than a long hall with a few pews. Near the entrance, a young man wearing a simple homespun robe and wool gloves lies sleeping on a cot.*

Near his bed are several incense burners filling the chamber wi[th] a sweet, minty scent.

Down the aisle, slightly obscured by incense smoke, you see t[he] outline of a statue, and can hear the faint sounds of religio[us] chanting.

Sword Dak is an acolyte of Set, masquerading as a prie[st] of Mitra. He is currently feigning sleep to lure the PCs in[to] a false sense of security. Once he "awakens," he greets th[e] PCs and advises how the Weeping Maiden delivers her me[s]sage (50 gp per "yes" or "no" answer), "As per the ancie[nt] rhyme of Saint Hastor…":

*Five upon five and then again, the Maiden sets her price
Pilgrims travelling across the sands, will pay for Her advice
Wisdom sought is wisdom earned, her countenance will convey
If one considers wisdom delivered as solely Yay or Nay"*

Note: If a lawful cleric asks about Saint Hastor, a DC 14 Personality check rewards them with the knowledge that they are 99% sure they've never heard of a Saint Hastor. (Hastor was a cleric of Set that Avvani and Akken were friends with back in Mitra's Fist.)

When the PCs finally decide to investigate the statue, Sword Dak watches the PCs travel down the aisle and makes "ceremonial gestures" which actually signals the living statue to "awaken" and controls its eyes.

Sword Dak (wizard): Init +3; Atk short sword +3 melee (1d6+2); Crit I/d8; AC 12; HD 3d4+3 (hp 15); MV 30'; Act 1d20; SP immune to poison, spellcasting (+5 spell check): Spells (1st) *chill touch, color spray, comprehend languages, magic missile, magic shield, ventriloquism*; (2nd) *invisibility, phantasm*; SV Fort +2, Ref +3, Will +2; AL C.

Dak wears a eucalyptus lined robe which conceals his short sword and protects him from the desert salamanders. If attacked, Dak turns himself invisible and then orders the basalt maiden and chanting skeletons to cover his retreat before fleeing down the mountain (he has no risk of falling on the rocks as he is quite familiar with the cairn) and seeking the protection of his parents, Avvani and Akken. Sword Dak's spell book is hidden within one of the pews (easily found if players announce they are searching the benches).

Area 2-3 – Weeping Maiden: *In the center of the raised dais a dark-stoned statue carved roughly into the shape of a human woman. Her face is contorted into a scowl of grief, with creases stained from tears of blood. Next to the statue is an altar topped with several treasures left in offering. From behind a curtain on the west wall, the low sounds of rhythmic chanting can be heard.*

Basalt Maiden: This statue is actually a living stone statue created by Avvani, Akken, and Dak to swindle pilgrims out of their sacrificial offerings. Once the PCs place an offering on the table worth at least 50 gp, Sword Dak activates a *phantasm* spell making it appear as if her eyes have opened and are scanning the PCs. Sword Dak exclaims from down the hallway, *"It's a miracle! The Maiden will now hear your prayers!"*

Most of the treasure on the table is fake, but there is a single silver chalice worth 5 gp to fool any dwarves that may be in the party. Sword Dak encourages the PCs to offer more magic or treasure to have their prayers answered. If the PCs threaten him, attempt to take the offerings on the table, or make any overt attempt to see if the statue is fake, Sword Dak gives the basalt maiden the signal to attack.

Basalt maiden: Init +3; Atk fist +3 melee (1d8+2); Crit M/d10; AC 16; HD 4d8 (hp 28); MV 30'; Act 1d20; SP acid eye squirt, immune to poison and mind-affecting spells, half damage from cold; SV Fort +4, Ref -2, Will -2; AL N.

Acid eye squirt (2/day): The basalt maiden sprays a single target with red acid that shoots from its eyes. The acid squirt has an attack bonus of +1, a range of 30' and causes 1d5 points of damage (DC 12 Fortitude save for half damage).

Area 2-4 – Chanting Monks: *Behind the curtain, you are alarmed to discover the source of the chanting—four skeletons brandishing swords, their jawbones flapping disturbingly as they groan! The skeletons are stationed in front of an alabaster dome poking out from the rocks.*

The chanting is the result of a *ventriloquism* spell cast on the skulls of each of the skeletons. The skeletons attack if summoned by Sword Dak or if the PCs enter the area.

Chanting skeletons (4): Init +0; Atk short sword +0 melee (1d6) or claw +0 melee (1d3); Crit U/d6; AC 9; HD 1d6 (hp 4 each); MV 30'; Act 1d20; SP fear chant, un-dead traits, half damage from piercing and slashing weapons; SV Fort +0, Ref +0, Will +0; AL C.

Fear chant (1/day): The chanting skeletons transform their chant from harmless vocals into a frightful dirge. Any target within 30' must make a DC 12 Willpower save or experience fright. Frightened opponents immediately flee the area at maximum speed for 1d4+1 rounds. All the skeletons are chanting the same hymn, so the save only needs to be made once.

The chanting skeletons brandish short swords and wear shendyts adorned with unholy glyphs dedicated to Set.

Dome: Obvious to dwarves, and discernible by other PCs with a DC 10 Intelligence check, is that the dome is actually the top of a structure buried beneath the rocky cairn (the True Shrine of Mitra). The dome can be breached with a successful *planar step* spell, or via brute strength (at least two PCs cooperating, with both succeeding on a DC 15 Strength check to remove the capstone). Once removed, PCs can lower themselves 30' down to area 5-2 below (DC 10 Reflex save or fall for 2d6 falling damage if they fall while unsecured). See *The Sanctified Temple* sidebar in area 5-1 if characters of chaotic alignment attempt to enter the shrine.

AREA 3: GORGE & CAVERNS

See **Map 3: The Cairn**

Long before the arrival of the Mitraic apostles, this region was the lair and hunting grounds of the stone giant Gabbro. Being of neutral alignment, Gabbro permits the presence of the local factions assuming he is occasionally compensated with offerings of food or trinkets. Gabbro was paid handsomely by Avvani to bury the two shrines using his natural *transmute earth* ability. Despite that, he has no loyalty to her, nor to any followers of Mitra for that matter.

Area 3-1 – Gorge: *The path winds along the base of the hill before eventually opening into a gorge surrounded by steep rocky cliffs. Piled against the western wall of the gorge is a scree slope of stones. From the top of the slope, a narrow set of switchbacks wind their way up the face of the rock wall towards a cave mouth sixty feet above. Across the gorge to the east grows a grove of fragrant trees with trunks of white bark.*

The center of the ravine is littered with the bones and skins of pack animals. The carcasses appear to have been gnawed on by scavengers.

The bones are from camels, mules, and horses eaten by Gabbro and his pet bear.

Obvious to dwarves, and discernible to other PCs with a DC 10 Intelligence check, is that the gorge is actually a quarry. The scree slope was formed from debris being ejected from the cave entrance (area 3-2).

The trees are normal eucalyptus trees, the scent of which repels desert salamanders. However, collecting eucalyptus leaves aggravates a swarm of gall wasps which constructed their hive in the branches.

Gall wasp swarm: Init +5; Atk swarming bite +1 melee (1 plus sting [+1d3 damage, DC 5 Fort negates]); Crit N/A; AC 11; HD 4d8 (hp 24); MV fly 40'; Act special; SP bite all targets within 20' x 20' space, half damage from non-area attacks; SV Fort +0, Ref +10, Will -2; AL N.

Area 3-2 – Cave Entrance: *The switchbacks lead to a cave mouth sixty feet above the valley floor. The ledge is littered with scat from a large animal, and a large pile of boulders is stacked near the cave entrance.*

The scat is from the cave bear Talus which lives in area 3-3. Gabbro uses the stones for target practice and to throw at interlopers (or PCs attempting to flee).

Area 3-3 – Talus the Cave Bear: *Loose gravel and dried leaves cover the floor of this natural cavern. Curled up sleeping on a bed of eucalyptus leaves is an enormous bear with dusty gray fur.*

Talus is currently hibernating. Unless the PCs act belligerently, or Gabbro is threatened, Talus will remain asleep. [If] the PCs harm the bear in any way, Gabbro will emerge fro[m] area 3-4 to slaughter them all.

Talus (cave bear): Init +2; Atk claw +4 melee (1d4) and bi[te] +5 melee (1d6+2); Crit M/d10; AC 17; HD 3d8 (hp 20); M[V] 20', climb 10'; Act 2d20; SP charge; SV Fort +4, Ref +1, W[ill] +8; AL N.

Charge: Talus initiates combat with a powerful charge er[d]ing in its claw attack. In addition to granting a +2 atta[ck] bonus and a -2 AC penalty to Talus, the bear's target mu[st] make a DC 14 Reflex save or be knocked prone.

Area 3-4 – Gabbro the Stone Giant: *This sparse cave[rn] is lined with boulders and the floor is packed with gravel. Near o[ne] smoothed rock wall, stones have been arranged to create a lar[ge] flat table surrounded by enormous chairs. Atop the table is a lar[ge] leather sack.*

Gabbro is currently concealed in the cave, nestled agair[st] the southwest wall; his rough, rocky exterior and gray sk[in] provides natural camouflage. If the PCs search the walls, [he] is spotted on an opposed Intelligence check vs. Gabbro's camouflage bonus. Dwarves are awarded a +4 bonus to th[e] check if they are within 10' of Gabbro's location.

From his concealed location, Gabbro watches the PCs wi[th] interest. He has interacted with Avvani and Akken enoug[h] to realize that humankind can be a deceptively powerful. [If] the PCs attempt to take any of his belongings, he cries o[ut] in Giantish, "FLEE!" If the PCs attempt to manipulate hi[m] with the *potion of human control* found in area 1-2 and fail, [he] attacks and fights to the death. If the PCs engage in comb[at] with Gabbro, Talus awakens in 1d3+1 rounds (the bear [is] groggy from hibernating) to come to the giant's aid.

Gabbro has no loyalty to the residents of Mitra's Cross. [If] the PCs engage the giant without aggression, he agrees [to] barter. Gabbro happily provides the PCs with the know[l]edge and rumors he knows in exchange for wine or goo[ds] worth at least 40 gp. For the price of two "plump came[ls]" Gabbro allows the PCs to enter the concealed passage (ar[ea] 4-1) into the tunnels.

The leather sack contains several baubles Jicc has recen[tly] delivered on Avvani's behalf: 20 sp, a flute, and four bottl[es] of Weeping Maiden wine.

Hidden behind some rocks 18 feet above the cavern flo[or] is Gabbro's treasure: a fang from a young green drag[on] (worth 100 gp, and which can be used as a short sword; it [is] also effective against creatures that can only be hit by ma[gic] weapons), and a jade snake figurine worth 40 gp. Inscrib[ed] on the figurine is an inscription in Giantish: "For your [ef]forts in the Burial of the Twins."

Gabbro (stone giant): Init +1; Atk club +18 melee (3d8+1[0]) or hurled stone +10 missile fire (1d8+10, range 200'); C[rit] 20-24 G/d4; AC 17; HD 12d10 (hp 72); MV 40'; Act 1d24; [SP] infravision 60', stone camouflage, *transmute earth*; SV F[ort] +12, Ref +6, Will +8; AL N.

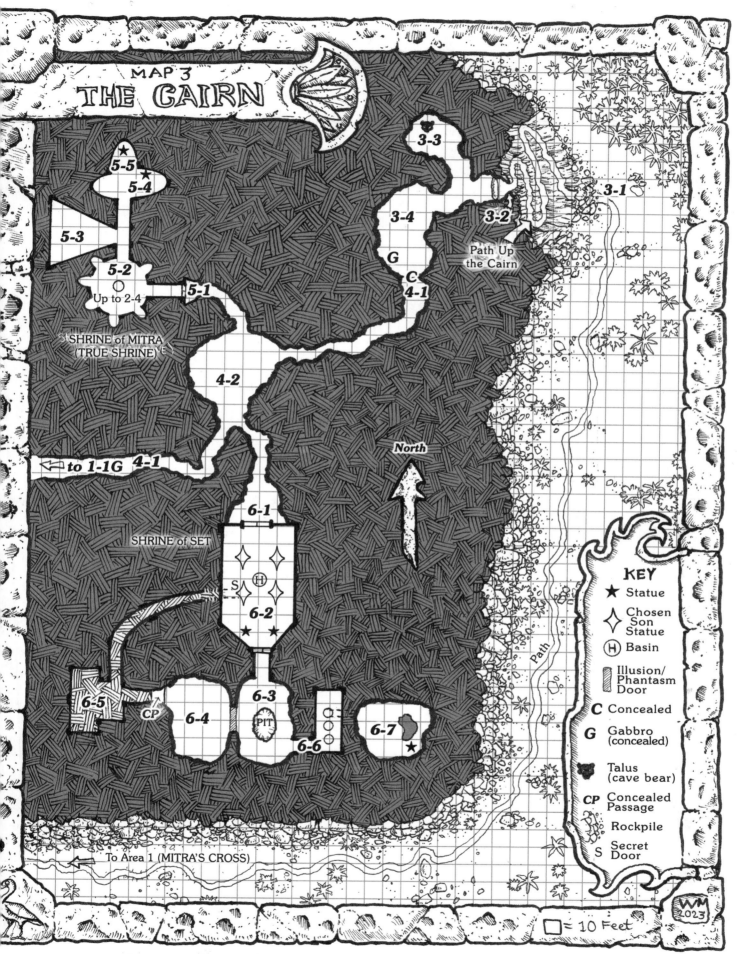

MAP 3
THE CAIRN

5-5
5-4
5-3
5-2
Up to 2-4
5-1

3-3
3-4
G
C
4-1
3-2
Path Up
the Cairn
3-1

SHRINE of MITRA
(TRUE SHRINE)

4-2

← to 1-1G   4-1

North

6-1

SHRINE of SET

S
H
6-2

6-5
CP
6-4
6-3
PIT
6-6
6-7

← To Area 1 (MITRA'S CROSS)

KEY

★ Statue

◈ Chosen
Son
Statue

H Basin

Illusion/
Phantasm
Door

C Concealed

G Gabbro
(concealed)

Talus
(cave bear)

CP Concealed
Passage

Rockpile

S Secret
Door

Path

□ = 10 Feet

WM
2023

Stone camouflage: Gabbro's gray, rocky exterior grants him +5 bonus on any attempt to hide while near natural stone or earthen walls.

Transmute earth (3/day): As per the 4th-level wizard spell (+6 spell check).

AREA 4: BENEATH THE CAIRN

See **Map 3** for the layout of the tunnels and shrines of Mitra and Set buried under the rock cairn.

Area 4-1 – Cavern: *A narrow tunnel has been bored straight into the rocks beneath the cairn. The tunnel does not appear natural nor does it have the appearance of being carved by humans or dwarves. Indeed, the rock walls appear melted and re-formed.*

The tunnel has not been mined (in the way that humankind might think of mining), but rather magically transformed via Gabbro's innate ability to *transmute earth*.

Area 4-2 – Battleground: *The tunnel eventually opens into a spacious cavern. The remnants of a skirmish between two factions litters the ground. One group was composed of snake-like humanoids, while their opponents were half-man/half-lion creatures. Both sides were equipped with crude tools and armor. Given the number of slain, it is unclear which side was the victor. High-pitched animal squeaking can be heard echoing from the cavern walls.*

This is where the snakefolk and the leonids periodically face off in their perpetual war. Skirmishes have been occurring

for centuries, and upon examination, it appears some of th[e] corpses were killed within the last few months, while other[s] are nothing more than bleached bones.

Searching for loot will startle the four carrion possums feed[-]ing on the corpses.

Carrion possum (4): Init +0; Atk bite +1 melee (1d3 plus p[oi-]son [+1d3 damage, DC 10 Fort negates]); Crit M/d6; AC 1[?] HD 1d6 (hp 3); MV 30', climb 10', burrow 10'; Act 1d20; S[P] playing possum; SV Fort +1, Ref +2, Will -2; AL N.

Playing possum: When a carrion possum reaches 0 hit poin[ts] it gains a single additional attack against any creature wit[h-]in 5' before permanently expiring.

Carrion possums are gray, hairless, cat-sized creatures ofte[n] mistaken for cave rats. They can be found in almost all env[i-]ronments and gained their name from their surprise attac[k] when presumed dead.

Searching for loot requires a successful Luck check (ma[xi-]mum of one item found per PC):

TABLE 1: BATTLEGROUND LOOT

1d5	Loot Found
1	Usable leonid shield (provides +1 bonus to AC). Inscribed on the shield is the sigil "Clan of the Green Breath" (a clue for area 6-6).
2	1d3 javelins
3	Rot grub infested leonid corpse!
	Rot grub: Init (always last); Atk burrow +0 mele[e] (special); Crit N/A; AC 10; hp 1; MV N/A; Ac[t] 1d20; SP burrow; SV Fort +0, Ref -4, Will +2; AL N.
	Burrow: On a successful attack, the grub burrow[s] into the PC's flesh, working its way toward the[ir] heart in 1d4+2 rounds. Digging out the grub re[-]quires a DC 15 Agility check, causing 1 point o[f] damage per attempt. Barbers, surgeons, and other[s] PCs with a medical background receive a +2 bonus to the check. If the grub isn't removed in time, i[t] burrows into the victim's heart, resulting in instan[-]taneous death.
4	*Potion of healing* (see DCC RPG p. 224) hidden on a snakefolk warrior.
5	Carrion cave crab swarm! Rolling over the corpse of a snakefolk reveals a patch of a carrion crabs feasting on the body.
	Cave crab swarm: Init +0; Atk swarming pincers +1 melee (1d3); Crit M/d6; AC 10; HD 1d8 (hp 3[?]) MV 20', climb 10', burrow 10'; Act special; SP pinch all targets with a 10' x 10' space, half damage from non-area attacks; SV Fort +0, Ref +6, Will -2; AL N.
	Cave crabs are fist-sized subterranean cousins to their well-known saltwater kin. They have the innate ability to burrow through soil and rock in their search for decaying matter.

AREA 5: TRUE SHRINE OF MITRA

Area 5-1 – Outside Shrine: The following text assumes the PCs are approaching from the caverns to the east.

The narrow tunnel ends at a wall of flawless alabaster. Set into this facade is a bronze door adorned with a script which sparkles like starlight. You now have no doubt that the cairn and tunnels are not natural, but that someone, or something, has deliberately buried a magnificent structure.

The bronze door is inscribed with magic runes which can be deciphered with a *read magic* or *detect magic* spell. The deciphered transcription reads:

Almighty and just Mitra, You are the lion. We give You thanks for smiting the unholy Set and mauling his wickedness. May Your righteousness and the Maiden's law protect those who seek respite in this shrine sanctified in Your name by Your humble servant Knight Graydon.

The bronze door is not locked, but entering the shrine can be hazardous to PCs of chaotic alignment (see sidebar **The Sanctified Temple**).

Area 5-2 – Hall of Heroes: *This cylindrical chamber is capped with a domed ceiling thirty feet above your heads. The dome's keystone is inscribed with the sigil of Mitra.*

Spaced evenly around the walls are six alcoves. Within each niche is a desiccated corpse propped upright in a fighting pose. The corpses are of various races and possessions — some bear armor and weapons, and others are adorned in spellcaster robes. Above each alcove, a plaque displays the name of the inhabitant in archaic lettering. Five of the six niches have a torch burning above them.

A pleasant, earthy smell fills the chamber, drifting from a small incense burner in the corner of the chamber.

The torches above the burial niches are magical and continuously burn while in the Shrine—they cannot be extinguished by normal means, but only by manipulating the incense burner (or via *dispel magic*). Characters examining the incense burner notice it has six holes, only five of which discharge smoke; the hole corresponding to niche #2 has been covered. Covering one of the holes on the burner extinguishes the torch above the corresponding alcove. Disturbing one of the bodies without first blocking its correspond-

ing hole on the incense burner summons two angelic pumas. The angelic pumas have animal-intelligence and therefore cannot be negotiated with. If they have been triggered, they attack on sight.

Angelic puma (2): Init +2; Atk bite +3 melee (1d5+1 plus bite grapple) and claw +2 melee (1d4); Crit DN/d4; AC 12; HD 2d10 (hp 20, 16); MV 30', climb 20'; Act 1d20; SP bite grapple; SV Fort +2, Ref +3, Will +1; AL L.

Bite grapple: If an angelic puma lands a successful bite attack, the target will be held in the puma's locked jaws (DC 13 Strength check to escape). The target will then take 1d3 points of damage each round until it escapes.

Angelic pumas have the sleek body of a puma with black fur shimmering with points of glowing purple like fireflies.

The niches contain disciples of Mitra. Each corpse is adorned in funeral pageantry befitting their rank with at least 3d5 gp worth of jewelry, in addition to the items listed below:

1. "Golddar Gullbladder": male dwarf, battleaxe (missing one finger)
2. "Bree Felkner": female human (missing four fingers), scale mail armor. Initially, this niche has no torch burning above it.
3. "Aalina Softwind": female elf, shortbow
4. "Brock the Fair": male human, cleric, holy symbol of Mitra
5. "Strongrowl": male leonid, short sword (missing a fang, and an ear)
6. "Lucky Luce": female halfling, leather armor (missing front teeth)

If the dome is breached, PCs gain access to area 2-4.

Area 5-3 – Field of Leonids: *The entire west wall of this chamber has been decorated with an incredibly realistic painting depicting half-man/half-lion creatures sparring on fields of fiery-red grass beneath an unnatural golden sky. The artist has meticulously captured how the beast men fight with swords, shields, javelins, and sometimes their teeth!*

In the center of the room is a pedestal holding a stone mortar and pestle set, both of which are dusted with a fine white powder.

PCs with background occupations of butcher, grave digger, healer, or wizard's apprentice recognize the powder as crushed bones and/or animal fangs (leonids).

Extracting a bone from any of the heroes in area 5-2 and crushing it in the bowl teleports 2d5 leonid warriors from a secluded pocket of the Overworld. Once conjured, the leonids expect to be led to battle against the forces of Chaos within 2d3 turns or they will turn on their summoners and return through the painting to their homeworld.

Leonid warrior (varies): Init +1; Atk short sword +3 melee (1d6+1) or bite +2 melee (1d6) or javelin +2 missile fire (1d6, range 30'); Crit II/d6; AC 14 (hide); HD 2d8 (hp 14 each); MV 30'; Act 1d20; SP fearful roar; SV Fort +1, Ref +1, Will +1; AL L.

THE SANCTIFIED TEMPLE

The Temple of Mitra was *sanctified* (as per the cleric spell) by Knight Graydon over 600 years ago upon completion of its construction. This makes the area dangerous to PCs of chaotic alignments. A chaotic PC who enters any area of the shine must make a DC 28 Fortitude save or take 1d5 points of damage upon entry, an additional 1 point of damage each turn they remain in the shrine thereafter, and makes all rolls at a -1d penalty while in the shrine.

"What force rules over humans created by the whims of humans?"

Answering the riddle incorrectly has no consequences; th custos castor merely shakes its rodentlike head in disa pointment and says, "Alas, yet another who is unworthy."

If the PC answers "Law" the custos castor excitedly pr claims, "Correct! And from this day until the day your ques is complete, you shall be known as The Toothbearer!" Th guardian then flaps its tiny wings and cries out, "By Mitra' Bones, you shall be fortified with His strength to smite Set' evil!" The guardian then casts a derivative of *planar ste* which dissolves the PCs' teeth (causing 1 point of damag no save) and replaces them with *Mitra's Jaws of Law* (see A pendix B).

The custos castor allows lawful PCs to pass unmolested they choose not to answer the riddle. Chaotic PCs are c fered the opportunity to "Repent their sinful ways and er brace the purity that comes from Mitra's truth!" Any chaoti PC that attempts to leave without first repenting, or any P that attempts to abscond with the holy teeth without firs solving the riddle, faces the custos castor's wrath.

Custos castor (angelic servant, Law): Init +2; Atk claw + melee (1d4+2) or bite +3 melee (1d6+2); Crit 19-20 DN/d AC 13; HD 2d8+2 (hp 17); MV 20', fly 20'; Act 2d20; SP ange traits, cleric abilities ((+4 spell check): lay on hands, turn u holy), spellcasting (+4 spell check): Spells (1st) *blessing, detec evil, holy sanctuary, protection from evil;* (2nd) *banish, resto vitality;* SV Fort +4, Ref +1, Will +4; AL L.

Angel traits: Communication by speech or telepathy, ha damage from non-magical weapons, fire, acid, cold, electri ity, gas, can teleport back to native plane or any point o same plane, as long as not bound or otherwise summone can project astrally and ethereally, infravision 120', spe casting (+16 spell check): Spells (1st) *cantrip.*

The custos castor resembles a giant beaver with sparklin gold fur, tiny wings, and enormous incisors.

Area 5-5 – Maiden of Heart of Law: *The entire surfac of this domed alcove has been painted to depict the epic battle whe Mitra defeated the snake-demon Set over one thousand years ag under a blood red moon!*

In the center of the alcove rises a magnificent eight-foot-ta statue in the shape of a beautiful human female. The sta ue's face is water stained, making it appear as though sh has been recently crying. In the center of the statue's che where the woman's heart should be is an empty hollow d pression. Engraved on the pedestal beneath the statue is th inscription, "The Maiden of the Heart of Law." A small tabl at the edge of the niche holds about a dozen unlit praye candles.

This is the original "Weeping Maiden" statue which ha been visited for centuries by Mitraic priests and pilgrim hoping to bear witness to its miracles.

If the statue is vandalized, a *bolt from the blue* (as per the spe 1d12+14 spell check) strikes out at the defiler from the storr clouds painted on the dome above.

Fearful roar (1/day): The leonid warrior releases a loud intimidating roar. All opponents within 30' of the leonid must make a DC 13 Will save or experience fright. Frightened opponents immediately flee the area at maximum speed for 1d3 rounds.

Leonid warriors resemble human/lion hybrids who walk and fight on either two or four legs. They wear specially designed armor which keeps their weapons strapped to their backs when not in combat.

Area 5-4 – Mitra Alcove: *In the center of this alcove is a seven-foot-tall marble statue perched atop a three-foot-high pedestal of a male human warrior heroically wielding a sword. The statue has an unusual feature, as the man's head has been formed without lips or a mouth — instead, there is just a cantaloupe-sized cavity in the carving's face containing an incomplete set of teeth, yellowed with age and held together with a thin band of mithril. Engraved on the pedestal are the words "St. Mitra."*

Resting on a bed of straw in front of the statue is a giant rodent the size of a bear with golden fur and tiny wings. Protruding from its mouth is an imposing set of orange incisors.

The statue contains Mitra's actual teeth, harvested from his corpse by his apostles. The apostles have also conjured an angelic servant to monitor the artifact.

The guardian offers one PC "the blessings of the divine artifact to any servant worthy of Mitra who can answer the riddle of the custos castor!" (Typically, this would be a lawful PC, but the judge may allow the offering to a neutral PC if it suits their campaign.)

The statue bestows a miracle upon any lawful PC who lights a candle, prays to the Maiden, and makes a DC 15 Personality check (maximum of one miracle per PC per lifetime). Upon success, tears of blood appear on the statue's face as she bestows one of her gifts (roll 1d4 plus the PC's Luck modifier):

TABLE 2: THE MAIDEN'S BLESSING

Roll	Miracle Bestowed
1 or less	Holy Vision: The PC may ask one question similar to *second sight* (as per the spell, 1d8+10 spell check).
2	Cured! The character may call upon the maiden to heal one PC, as per *neutralize poison or disease* or *remove curse* (1d8+12 spell check).
3	The Corpse Whisperer: The PC may call upon the Maiden to help them *speak with the dead* (as per the spell, 1d8+15 spell check) at some point in the future.
4	Courage of Mitra: The PC gains a one-time +2 bonus to all attack rolls or spell checks when fighting un-dead or creatures associated with Set.
5+	Favor of Mitra: The Maiden kisses the PC's forehead, permanently bestowing 1 point of Strength and 1 point of Stamina (not to exceed 18).

Once the Maiden bestows a miracle, she proclaims, "By Mitra's Bones, in compensation for these gifts, you shall reward our faith by smiting the scourge of Set!" She then demands the PC embark on a holy quest determined randomly using the following table (or chosen by the judge):

TABLE 3: THE MAIDEN'S QUEST

1d3	Holy Quest
1	"Return to me my heart before the rising of the 12th full moon!"
	The PC has a full year to locate and return her missing Heart of Law (detailed in the DCC RPG adventure *Dark Tower*).
2	"Before the next full moon, find those who have unnaturally prolonged their life with Set's venom and force them to submit to the true age of Law!"
	The PC has a month to determine which of the NPCs' lives have been unnaturally prolonged (Avvani, Akken, Dakkar) and either dispatch them or destroy the source of their power (the *Fang of Set*).
	Note: This could also be used as an adventure hook to seek out the NPCs in the DCC RPG adventure *Dark Tower*.
3	"Before the next full moon, restore this Shrine to its rightful place under the sun's grace!"
	The PC has a month to figure out how to unbury this shrine from the cairn. It's left up to the judge on how this might be accomplished, but one method would be to entice Gabbro to use his powers to demolish the cairn he himself built.

AREA 6: SHRINE OF SET

Area 6-1 – Shrine of Set: *The tunnel terminates at a wide chamber encasing a finished wall of polished black stone. In the center of the wall are two gleaming black doors of tourmaline with brass handles. Etched in the doors' surfaces are golden images of giant reptilian creatures slaughtering and devouring humans. Glowing red glyphs beneath the images dimly illuminate the area with their sickly, blood-colored light.*

The tourmaline double doors are etched with magic runes which can be deciphered with a *read magic* or *detect magic* spell. The deciphered transcription reads:

"Behold! Almighty Set, Father of the Four Chosen Sons. You are the Lion's dread. May your venom cleanse this and all worlds of its mongrels."

The double doors are not locked, but are trapped (DC 15 *find trap*). The trap can be disabled with a DC 15 *disable trap* or by saying the phrase "Wherever the cur rises, so shall your sons" (the last stanza of the prayer found on Set's holy symbol in area 1-2) before opening the door. Failure to disarm the trap causes all creatures within 10' of the door to be zapped with electricity for 2d4 damage (DC 12 Fortitude save for half damage).

Area 6-2 – Hall of Chosen Sons: *This grand hall has floors and walls of polished black obsidian. The roof the chamber is supported by four fifteen-foot-tall columns ornately carved into grotesque otherworldly demons. While each of the creatures is unique, they all share a mixture of humanoid, draconic, and reptilian features. The columns also bear inscriptions written in a bilious language.*

Between the four columns stands a great brass basin, covered in vile images of snakes and dragons subjugating humans to profane acts of torture. The basin radiates heat, and smoldering embers rise upwards like fireflies. Carved in Common upon the basin is the message, "The Chosen Sons of Set demand tribute."

An arched passageway to the south is flanked by a pair of six-foot-tall statues depicting two-armed snake creatures brandishing weapons, their reptilian faces carved into angry scowls.

Each of the columns represents a Chosen Son of Set (Manahath, Caphet, Ophois, and Skabhet). Their common names—no one would dare carve a demon's true name—are inscribed in both Serpent and Demonic. A secret panel in the Manahath column (DC 15 Intelligence check to locate) provides access to a tunnel leading to area 6-5.

The snake statues flanking the southern doors monitor whoever enters the chamber to ensure they make an offering worthy of the Chosen Sons. The statues' eyes follow the PCs movements and their faces appear to scowl. As the PCs deposit funds or magic into the basin, their scowls soften, eventually transforming into passive indifference once the appropriate tribute is met. Offerings placed in the basin do not melt.

Inside the basin are smoldering embers which radiate heat. If the PCs attempt to exit the chamber without first leaving at least 100 gp worth of goods (or a magic item) in the basin, the chamber's guardians attack. An elemental formed from the embers rises from the basin while the statues attack with spells. The western statue creates a choking cloud and the eastern statue spits magic missiles.

Leaving an offering for a Chosen Son of Set is considered an unholy act. Any lawful cleric present when the offering is made must make a Luck check, with failure resulting in the cleric rolling 2d4 on the deity disapproval table (see DCC RPG p. 122).

Smoldering embers elemental: Init +3; Atk slam +3 melee (1d6+2); Crit M/d8; AC 14; HD 3d8 (hp 21); MV 30'; Act 1d20; SP smoldering spray, immune to fire, vulnerable to cold (double damage); SV Fort +3, Ref -1, Will -1; AL C.

Smoldering spray (2/day): The elemental projects a cone of smoldering ash 30' long and 10' wide at its terminus. All creatures within the area of the spray must make a DC 12 Reflex save or take 1d6 damage.

Guardian snakefolk statue (2): Init +4 (surprise); Atk special; Crit N/A; AC 16; HD 3d8 (hp 20, 18); MV N/A; Act 1d20; SP surprises 50% of time, spellcasting (+3 spell check): spells (1st) *choking cloud, magic missile*; immune to critical hits; SV Fort +4, Ref -5, Will +3; AL N.

Area 6-3 – Pit of the Unworthy: *The walls of this space have been worked smooth into a rounded chamber. Your footsteps echo off the walls, and a deep unsettling breathing seemingly emanates from all around you. In the center of the chamber is a pit over twenty feet deep. At the bottom of the pit are several sets of humanoid, leonid, and reptilian remains slowly liquefying in a pool of foul-smelling brown goo.*

A passage to the southeast leads deeper into the temple.

The western wall has a *phantasm* cast upon it (a deliberate DC 18 Willpower save pierces the illusion), hiding the passage to area 6-4. The inhabitants of that area watch the PCs through the illusion and attack with surprise if the PCs manage to disbelieve the illusion or enter their lair. If the PCs leave the chamber without first discovering them, the snakefolk younglings will stalk the PCs and attempt an ambush once the PCs reach area 6-6.

The brown liquid at the bottom of the pit is a necrotic ooze which is slowly feeding on the decaying corpses of adventuring interlopers who have perished in the temple and a few snakefolk. Slowly being digested are the bodies of Acolytes Rupert and Chilton who can be identified via their intact holy symbols (which are immune to the effects of the ooze). If any PC comes within 5' of the bottom of the pit, the necrotic ooze lashes out with one of its pseudopods.

Necrotic ooze: Always last (after surprise); Atk pseudopod +3 melee (1d3 plus digestive acid [+1d3 damage, DC 13 Fort negates]); Crit M/d8; AC 10; HD 2d8 (hp 10); MV 5', climb 5'; Act 1d20; SP surprises 25% of time, stench, half damage from slicing and piercing weapons; SV Fort +6, Ref -8, Will -6; AL N.

Stench: Any creature that starts its initiative within 10 feet of the necrotic ooze must succeed on a DC 13 Fortitude save or becomes nauseous and suffers a -2 penalty to all rolls for 1d3 rounds.

Area 6-4 – Geb, Father of Snakes: If the PCs enter this chamber through area 6-3's illusionary wall, use the following read-aloud text. Otherwise, if they enter from the passage in area 6-5, the PCs gain surprise.

Stepping through the illusion of the false wall, you're startled as you come face to face with a giant snake as large as a tavern sitting on a pile of mucous-covered eggs. The horrific beast coils upon itself creating a repugnant grating sound as its scales rub together.

The creature lets out a long hiss, revealing an entire row of fangs the size of short swords. Peeking out from behind the beast's coils are four human-sized snakefolk. The demon seems to be giving birth to eggs and live young right in the chamber!

This monstrosity is one of the many incarnations of Geb, father of Snakes. Geb is bound to the chamber to excrete a never-ending stream of snakefolk younglings which, if not eaten by their father, depart the temple seeking out leonids to battle.

Concealed behind a pile of half-eaten snakefolk carcasses and eggshells is a long-forgotten passage leading to area 6-5.

Geb (giant green spitting cobra): Init +5; Atk bite +5 melee (2d4+2); Crit 19-20 G/d4; AC 14; HD 4d8 (hp 23); MV 40', climb 30'; Act 2d20; SP spit poison, cannibalistic, immune to poison; SV Fort +4, Ref +5, Will +2; AL C.

Spit poison (2/day): Geb is able to spit poison in a spray 30' long and 20' wide at its terminus. All creatures within the spray take 1d5 damage (DC 14 Fortitude save negates).

Cannibalistic: The ravenous Geb is sustained by consuming its young as they are birthed. There is a 30% chance on Geb's initiative count that, instead of attacking a PC, it will attempt to swallow one of its snakefolk younglings.

Geb is a giant snake, over 40' long when fully uncoiled. Geb excretes both live young and eggs at a rate of 1d3 every 3rd round, the majority of which it then consumes.

Snakefolk youngling (4): Init +0; Atk bite +1 melee (1d5 plus poison [+1d3 damage, DC 13 Fort negates]) or claw +1 melee (1d4); Crit M/d6; AC 11; HD 1d8 (hp 5 each); MV 30', climb 20'; Act 1d20; SP infravision 60', immune to poison; SV Fort +0, Ref +1, Will -2; AL C.

The snakefolk younglings are snake-like humanoids with spindly arms and glowing orange eyes.

Area 6-5 – Unviable Offspring: *Feathery cobwebs fill this chamber, giving the appearance that no one has visited this part of the temple in decades. Long forgotten and covered in dust are two infant-sized sarcophagi covered in runes. One of the coffins has been bound closed with an ancient desiccated skin of a giant snake.*

On a small table near the coffins are several black candles and two small clay jars, one of which has been broken open.

A narrow passage filled with cobwebs leads to the east, and a larger passage exits north.

Dwarves in the party can smell precious metal emitting from Aphis' sarcophagus.

Clerics in the party examining the candles and jars can make a DC 12 Personality check to recognize the items as ceremonial elements required for divine rituals related to healing, removing corruption, and resurrection.

The runes on the coffin are written in Demonic.

The first coffin bears an ibis symbol and the inscription, "Akkar: Born of Set's high priests Akken and Avvani. Twin brother of Dakkar". Inside the coffin is an infant-sized mummy. Unwrapping the mummy reveals that the baby had lizard-like reptilian legs protruding from a deformed torso clearly incompatible with life.

The second, snakeskin-wrapped coffin bears a viper symbol and the inscription, "Aphis: Born of Mahna, Son of Set, and the high priest Avvani". Removing the snakeskin and opening this coffin reveals the withered corpse of a leonid. Avvani sacrificed the leonid when she performed the resurrection ritual for her son Aphis using *Imhoptep's Rod of Resurrection* (see Appendix B). As required by the resurrection ritual, the rod is still in the coffin. To deter looters, Avvani has set an activation condition triggering the snake skin to animate and attack if the rod is removed from the coffin. If the PCs previously burned or destroyed the skin, then the largest fragment will grow larger and attack. Casting *detect evil* or *detect magic* on the rod reveals its nature and abilities.

More information on the NPC Aphis can be found in the DCC RPG adventure *Dark Tower*.

Snake skin ghoul: Init -2; Atk bite +3 melee (1d3 plus life-drain); Crit U/d8; AC 9; HD 3d8 (hp 19); MV 20'; Act 1d20; SP lifedrain, un-dead traits; SV Fort +4, Ref -4, Will +2; AL C.

Lifedrain: The snake skin ghoul's fangs are capable of draining its target of their lifeforce. Victims must make a DC 14 Fortitude save or temporarily lose 1d3 Stamina. If their Stamina reaches 0, the victim dies and will be resurrected as one of Geb's snakefolk younglings in 1d6 months (and most likely immediately eaten). Victims regain 1 point of Stamina per day.

Area 6-6 – Three Pools: *The corridor opens into a rectangular chamber thirty feet wide by twenty feet across. The walls are unnaturally black and the air is thick with a nauseating pale-green smoke making it difficult to breathe. The area appears empty save for three pools filled with churning water of different colors, one each of green, red, and blue.*

Any snakefolk younglings from area 6-4 stalking the PCs attempt a surprise attack here, trying to push whichever PC is closest into the red pool. The character can avoid being pushed into the pool by succeeding on an opposed Strength check against the snakefolk's +1 Strength check.

Upon closer inspection, what first appears to be roiling water in the pools is actually bubbling smoke (similar to dry ice "fog"). Each pool has different characteristics:

- Red pool: Radiates heat, is 10' deep, and is a fire trap. Inanimate objects thrown into the pool have no effect, but when living matter touches the pool, it causes a fiery explosion resulting in 1d8 damage to all within 10' of the pool (DC 12 Fortitude save for half damage). PCs who remain in the pool continue to take 1d8 damage each round on their initiative until rescued.

- Blue pool: Radiates cold, is 10' deep, and is a frost trap. This pool is inverse to the red pool—the blue smoke can be touched by living creatures without issue, but inanimate objects tossed into the pool ejects a blast of ice shards causing 1d6 damage to all standing within 15' of the pool (DC 12 Fortitude save for half damage).

- Green pool: Smells of rank earth. The smoke from this pool is harmless but limits vision to 10' (PCs with infravision are not affected). The pool is actually the top of a natural rock chimney with a 20' drop straight down into area 6-7. PCs can descend with a DC 10 *climb sheer surfaces* or by climbing down by rope (DC 12 Agility check to avoid 1d6 falling damage if they fall while unsecured).

Note: A thief can make a DC 10 *handle poison* check to collect a 1d3 samples of the red or blue smoke which can be bottled and later used as a weapon.

Area 6-7 – Mahna, Runt of Set: *The temperature cools as you descend into a cavern deeper underground. Along the walls several burning torches fill the chamber with green smoke which swirls around your heads and dimly illuminates the chamber. Shadowy figures obscured by the vapors stand at attention near the torches.*

Barely visible through the smoke, you see a stalagmite which has been exquisitely carved into a sculpture of a snake tightly co

stricting a struggling man and burying its fangs into the man's neck. The realism of the man's agony is palpable. It is obvious that the man represents Mitra and the snake is the demon Set. One of the fangs glows with magical energy.

As you examine the carving, a gigantic creature slowly emerges head-first from a pool of murky water in the eastern half of the cavern. The four-legged beast stands seven feet tall—a demonic cow with a head like a snout-less pig. The demon waves its great pate—which you notice has no eyes—sniffing the air around it before opening its giant maw and growlingly speaking in a deep, phlegmy voice:

"Are you underfed curs Mitra's sycophants, or has the ancient village crone finally worked up the courage to try to claim the Fang?" At the mention of the "Fang," the creature nods its ponderous head toward the carving.

The beast sniffs again, drawing in a deep stream of the green smoke before continuing, "I am weary of this life as a sentinel. This temple should have fallen decades ago. I long to join my chosen brothers at the true tower of my father."

This time when its jaws open wide, it roars.

Mahna is one of Set's innumerous Runts. Far from a Chosen Son, Set considers Runts mongrels, barely more worthy than a minion. The Runts are considered weaklings (relatively speaking compared to Chosen or Lesser Sons of Set) and are thus given menial tasks; in this case, guarding the *Fang of Set* housed in this insignificant temple.

Mahna is blind—hence why he is considered a Runt—but can perceive his environment through his acute sense of smell afforded by the torches' green smoke. Dousing two or more of the torches, or diluting their efficacy by creating other strong scents in the chamber (such as burning eucalyptus), causes Mahna to fight with a -4 penalty to attack rolls. Mahna has posted four snakefolk younglings to guard the torches. They fight with bows unless a PC approaches.

Mahna (demonoid Runt of Set): Init +1; Atk bite +4 melee (1d8+1 plus dismember); Crit DN/d4; AC 16; HD 4d12 (hp 40); MV 30', swim 30'; Act 2d20; SP dismembering bite, hyperosmia, demon traits; SV Fort +4, Ref +4, Will +0; AL C.

Dismembering bite: If Mahna succeeds on a bite attack, it can make another bite attack that same round to attempt to dismember its target. If the second bite attack succeeds, the target takes 1d4 damage and loses a limb; roll 1d4: (1) left arm (2) right arm; (3) left leg; (4) right leg. The victim continues to take 1d2 points of damage each round thereafter until healing is applied.

Hyperosmia: Mahna requires the green smoke to "see." Dousing two or more torches, or creating a distracting scent, results in Mahna incurring a -4 penalty to attack rolls.

Demon traits: Communication by speech, half damage from non-magical weapons or natural attacks from creatures of 2 HD or less, half damage from fire, acid, cold, electricity, and gas.

Mahna resembles a large, eyeless hippopotamus covered in snake-like scales.

Snakefolk youngling (4): Init -2; Atk bite +1 melee (1d4 plus poison [+1d3 damage, DC 13 Fort negates]) or claw + melee (1d4) or bow +0 missile fire (1d6; range 60'); Crit M/ d6; AC 11; HD 1d8 (hp 5 each); MV 30', climb 20'; Act 1d20; SP infravision 60', immune to poison; SV Fort +0, Ref + Will -2; AL C.

The Carving: The carving is called "Set Conquering Mitra" and was carved by the demon artist Khufu after the temple's consecration. The glowing fang in the snake statue is the *Fang of Set* (see Appendix B), one of Set's actual teeth taken from his mortal demon body after his defeat by Mitra. The fang is an unholy artifact revered by Set's chaotic priests and Mahna has spent the last 300 years guarding it. Any lawful PC attempting to remove the fang without a cleric's *protection from evil* or a *blessing* is targeted by a *bolt from the blue* (as per the spell, 1d12+14 spell check) striking out at the vandal from the head of the carved snake. The PC removing the fang has a quick vision of a giant snake thousands of years old, coiled around a black tower. The snake looks at the PC and says, "My sons await you at the tower…" before opening its maw and striking out with phantasmal bite inflicting 2d6 damage (DC 13 Willpower save for half damage).

ENDING THE ADVENTURE

his adventure should provide several motivations for the PCs to want to visit Mitra's Fist and uncover the secrets of the two towers:

- If Avvani, Akken, or Dakkar still live at the end of the adventure, they become aware if the PCs recover the *Fang of Set* through divine channeling. Knowing they must stay within 5 miles of the artifact lest they begin their unnatural aging, they (along with Jicc and Rahkert if they still live) join forces and follow the PCs at a discreet distance until they can find an ideal time to ambush the party and recover the *Fang*. Ornery judges may also consider

a second "boss fight" ambush initiated by the denizens of Mitra's Cross when the PCs emerge from the beneath the cairn.

- Any PC bestowed with a miracle by the Maiden receives reminders to make progress on their holy quest every time they use, or are cured by, divine magic.

- The *Fang of Set* is a dangerous, unholy artifact and lawful deities encourage whichever PC has it in their possession to take it to Holomir Goldheart in the White Tower (see the DCC RPG adventure *Dark Tower*). Holomir will know how it can be destroyed.

APPENDICES
APPENDIX A: DRAMATIS PERSONAE

Character	Background & Motives	Knowledge/Rumors
Akken ("Ken")	• Priest of Set and former resident of Mitra's Fist. He is brother to Avvani, and has a complex relationship blaming her for the two of them becoming stranded in Mitra's Cross. Regardless, as his only long-term companion over the centuries, he has fathered two children with her (Dakkar and the late Akkar) and immediately comes to her aid if she is threatened. • Akken witnessed the aging effects when trying to leave Mitra's Cross without the *Fang* and doesn't want to age like Avvani has. • Currently shares a home with his (uncursed) companion Rahkert. • Ultimately Akken would also like to leave Mitra's Cross, and would attempt to retrieve the *Fang of Set* from any party that brings it out from under the cairn.	• People in this region will tattoo themselves with symbols that represent their children.
Acolyte Bentley	• Priest of Mitra. Was drugged by Avvani shortly before arrival so never actually laid his eyes on the true temple. • Suspects that something is amiss with the temple, but "hasn't had the strength to visit the great monument himself in some time."	• The Temple houses the statues of the Divine Bicameral: Mitra and the Maiden • The bones of saints are powerful magic! They are as deadly as any blacksmith's weapons, and when crushed in arcane rituals can conjure allies from the Overworld! • A similar temple dedicated to The Maiden exits in the small town of Mitra's Fist approximately 45 leagues away in the middle of Redmoon Pass. • Sadly, wherever a temple of Mitra appears, the forces of Set also typically establish an "unholy opposite."

Character	Background & Motives	Knowledge/Rumors
Avvani ("Vani")	• Priestess of Set, former resident of Mitra's Fist (see the DCC RPG adventure *Dark Tower*). Avvani has been a resident of Mitra's Cross for 300 years since her arrival to consecrate the Temple of Set with her brother Akken. • Short term motives: Coax town visitors to visit the false shrine and leave offerings which she gathers and shares with Jicc. • Long term motives: Searching for a way to "cheat" the curse of Set's Immortality so she can return to her estranged husband Avvakris back in Mitra's Fist. She believes possessing the *Fang of Set* would allow her to travel beyond the temple area without aging. • Avvani appears to be about 90 years old, as she has tried to escape town several times without the *Fang*, dramatically aging each time before returning. • "Late" wife of Avvakris of Mitra's Fist (see the DCC RPG adventure *Dark Tower*). Children with Avvakris: Avvaar, Avvala • She bore Mahna's son, Aphris, who died at birth. She later resurrected Aphris (see area 6-5) and he is being raised by her husband Avvakris back in Mitra's Fist. • Has a strained, complex relationship with her brother, Akken, as he has been her primary companion for the last 300 years. Nonetheless, she has borne him two children: Dakkar and Akkar (deceased).	• The temple on the cairn was built by the priests of Mitra over 600 years ago, and contains a statue called the "Weeping Maiden" which performs miracles if you leave an offering of wealth. (FALSE) • If asked about Rupert & Chilton: "Two priests came to visit a while back. They had dinner but didn't stay. They said they were going to pay a quick visit to the shrine and then attend some important business in Mitra's Fist. I haven't seen them since." (FALSE) • "Safest time to visit the shrine is in the morning at sunrise—that's when The Maiden speaks… Also, the crawlers aren't as active in the morning." (FALSE; this is when the desert salamanders are most active)
Dakkar ("Sword Dak")	• The son of Avvani and Akken, Dakkar is in on his mother's false temple scam and masquerades as a "Priest of the Maiden." • Is an accomplished illusionist. • Had a twin brother, Akkar, who died during childbirth. • Wears gloves, as one of his hands is a three-fingered reptilian lizard claw. • Has enjoyed his life in Mitra's Cross scamming the pilgrims. He is aware of his mother's longing to return to her estranged husband Akkaris, but has no interest in meeting his stepfather.	• Dakkar is always "in character," so he will only ever convey what it takes to "activate" the false maiden.
Gabbro	• 800-year-old stone giant who has lived in the area long before any of the other NPCs arrived. • Motives: Protect his cave bear and eat the occasional camel.	• Gabbro was paid by Avvani and Akken over 150 years ago to bury Mitra's Temple in a mountain of stone. He was happy to bury "both the temple of Law as well it's evil twin dedicated to Set" in order to keep The Balance. • The forces of Mitra and Set continue to skirmish in caverns that run under the mountain.

Character	Background & Motives	Knowledge/Rumors
Jicc	• Has worked for Avvani for over 15 years, but has been subject to so many of her spells that he has become mentally impaired. • Motives: Do whatever Avvani asks of him, lest he get slapped around. • Despite his fear of Avvani (and he is willing to gossip about her affairs), he is also fiercely protective of her and will fight to the death if she is threatened.	• Vani makes Jicc deliver a "nightcap" each night to the priest and a "pick me up" each morning. The "pick me up" doesn't seem to do much good as the priest just sleeps at the table all day. • "On the other side of the mountain above the gorge lives a 'stone man.' He's nice, especially if you bring him things to eat like wine or camels." Jicc has also heard Vani say there's a secret entrance into the mountain through the stone man's cave.
Rahkert ("Rah")	• Akken's companion. Knows that Akken is a priest of Set, but Rahkert is not under the confines of Set's Immortality. • Motive: Live a quiet life as a camel herder, and protect Akken if he is threatened.	• In this region, there are many towns named after Mitra (Mitra's Cross, Mitra's Bane, Mitra's Fist, Mitra's Curse, etc.) • People in this region will tattoo themselves with symbols that represent their children. Those symbols in an ankh represent children who have since died. • If asked about Rupert and Chilton: "Priests of Mitra come here all the time to visit the Weeping Maiden. They rarely stay long after they receive their divine guidance."

APPENDIX B: NEW MAGIC ITEMS

MITRA'S JAWS OF LAW

[Mi]tra's Jaws of Law is a religious artifact of a nearly com[pl]ete set of ancient yellow teeth bound together by a band [of] mithral. The teeth once resided in the mouth of Mitra and [we]re extracted by his apostles after his death. They were [br]ought to the new shrine of Mitra over 600 years ago as a [fea]ture to attract followers.

[If p]ossessed by a lawful cleric, the *Jaws* can be used as a holy [sy]mbol, and provide a +1 bonus to the cleric's spell checks [an]d class abilities. The artifact's greater powers are realized [wh]en a guardian angel of Mitra replaces a follower's own [te]eth with the *Jaws*. PCs who replace their teeth are thereaf[ter] addressed as "The Toothbearer" by any follower of Mitra.

[To] activate the *Jaws'* divine properties, the Toothbearer must [cr]y out, "By Mitra's Bones!" followed by a desired effect or [in]tent (e.g., "By Mitra's Bones, meet thy doom!" or "By Mi[tra']s Bones, thou shalt feel my wrath!"). The teeth can be [im]planted into any PC who is a follower of Mitra, but only [cle]rics receive the bonus to their spell checks and abilities.

[Wh]en implanted in the mouth of a lawful PC, the *Jaws of Law* [ha]ve the following characteristics:

[• +]2 bonus to cleric spell checks and abilities for clerics of Mitra.

• The teeth will communicate with their host via simple urges—typically urging the host to hurry up and smite the followers of Set, which is the artifact's primary goal.

• *Bite of glory*: The teeth provide the host with a +1 bite attack inflicting 1d4+1 damage. This attack is also effective against creatures that can only be hit by silver or magical weapons.

• *Detect evil* (1/day): The teeth allow the host to *detect evil* (as per the spell, 1d12+11 spell check).

• *Word of command* (1/day): The teeth allow the host to invoke a *word of command* (as per the spell, 1d12+11 spell check). Of course, the word must be preceded with, "By Mitra's Bones…"

• *Speak with the dead* (1/week): The teeth allow the host to *speak with the dead* (as per the spell, result 22-23).

FANG OF SET

The *Fang of Set* is a short sword constructed from a tooth dislodged from the mouth of Set during his final battle with Mitra. Retrieved from the battlefield, the tooth itself is 11" long and has been forged into a weapon to smite the followers of Mitra and Law.

The *Fang of Set* is a +1 short sword with the following characteristics:

- A successful attack poisons the target, inflicting 1d3 additional damage (DC 14 Fortitude save negates).

- The sword can communicate with its wielder telepathically using the Serpent language. The sword also enables its wielder to speak and understand the Serpent language.

- The sword's goal is to smite followers of Mitra. The wielder gains a +2 bonus to attack rolls and damage rolls when fighting opponents allied with Mitra.

- *Animal summoning (snakes)* (1/day): The sword allows the wielder to summon snakes (as per the spell, 1d12+11 spell check).

- *Set's immortality*: Characters wielding the *Fang* whose souls are pledged to Set benefit from *Set's immortality*, negating the effects of natural aging as long as they remain within 5 miles of the Fang. If the disciple travels beyond 5 miles from the location of the *Fang*, rapid aging begins at a pace of 1 "natural" year per hour (maximum of 200 hours) until the character reaches their true age (at which point the victim dissolves into dust). The aging stops if the disciple closes the gap between themselves and the *Fang*.

IMHOTEP'S ROD OF RESURRECTION

This rod is a 4' long oaken bough intricately carved into the shape of a walking stick entwined by a snake. It is a powerful religious item of clerics of Imhotep used in healing and resurrection rituals. While clerics of Imhotep gain additional bonuses, the *Rod* can be used by clerics of any alignment.

- *Imhotep's Rod of Resurrection* has the following characteristics:

- Can be used as a holy symbol for a cleric of Imhotep.

- Grants a +2 bonus to cleric spell checks and abilities for clerics of Imhotep.

- Can be used as a weapon (1d4 damage), and is effective against creatures affected only by silver or magic weapons.

Healing (1/day): The *Rod* heals 2 dice of damage as per the cleric's *lay on hands* ability.

- *Resurrection* (special): Clerics may perform a resurrection ritual for characters killed within the last 24 hours (and whose bodies are mostly intact) to be brought back to life with 1 hp. However, in order for the ritual to be successful, *another* person must be sacrificed and buried with the *Rod* on their corpse. If the *Rod* is removed from the body of the sacrificed victim, the resurrected person will immediately suffer 6d6 damage and 1d3 major corruptions (no save; see DCC RPG p. 118).

SET'S BOOTS OF THE SPITTING COBRA

The toes on these knee-high snakeskin boots have been formed into raised cobras poised to strike. The boots have the following characteristics:

- *Speed* (1/day): The wearer can move up to double the speed and gains an additional action die for 1d3 round

- *Spit venom* (1/day): Each boot can spit a caustic gob venom. The boots have an attack bonus of +3, a range 30', and cause 1d6 points of acid damage on a success hit (DC 14 Fortitude save for half damage).

SET'S DAGGER OF THE GAZING COBRA

When used in melee, this dagger shimmers with pulsati rainbow colors causing hypnosis to opponents.

- The dagger provides a +1 bonus to attack and damag rolls.

- *Snake climb* (1/day): The wielder can climb up walls like slithering snake at half their normal movement rate.

- *Hypnosis* (1/day per opponent): On a successful attac the victim must make a Willpower save vs. the dagge +3 spell check. Hypnotized opponents appear as if in daze and will perform tasks as commanded. Suicidal dangerous tasks negate the effect. The hypnosis fades ter 1d4 turns. Note: Set's offspring (including Mahna) a immune to this effect.

APPENDIX C: NEW SPELLS

INVISIBLE TO UNHOLY

Level: C1   **Range:** Varies   **Duration:** CL turns or permanent   **Casting Time:** 1 Action   **Save:** Will vs. spell check

General: The caster renders a mundane inanimate object or area invisible to unholy creatures.

Manifestation: None

	Failure.
-11	The cleric renders a mundane object (book, weapon, piece of equipment) invisible to unholy creatures for 1 turn per CL.
2-13	The cleric renders 1d3 objects invisible to unholy creatures for 1 turn per CL.
4-17	The cleric renders 1d3 + CL objects invisible unholy creatures for 1 turn per CL.
8-19	The cleric renders 1d3 + CL objects invisible to unholy creatures for 1d4 days plus 1 day per CL.
0-23	The cleric renders 1d3 + CL objects invisible to unholy creatures for 2d4 days plus 1 day per CL.
4-27	The cleric renders 1d3 objects invisible to unholy creatures permanently.
8-29	The cleric renders an entire area and all objects within that area (up to 10' x 10') invisible to unholy creatures for 1d8 days.
0-31	The cleric renders an entire area and all objects within that area (up to 20' x 20') invisible to unholy creatures for 2d6 + CL days.
2+	The cleric renders an entire area and all objects within that area (up to 20' x 20') invisible to unholy creatures permanently.

- MSutton -

Playtesters: Estella Castillo, Ava Newton, Stephen E. Paine, Santana the Fierce, Ashton Barstad, Alex Tausch, Cori Newton; Judge Matt "GrapeApe" Robertson: Shannon Kelley, Tim Sattley, Michael K. Dawson, Nathan Hackett (Harambear), Paul Davis, Ross Nyhan, Bruce Rusk; Judge Erica Lowe-Tarpley, Cliff Taylor, Brandon Clay, Damon Roman; Judge Stefan Surratt, Jeremy "Father Goose" Shuman Jr, Devin Watkins, Russell Bevers, Olivia "GuiltySP" De'Phantastiq, William Boxx; Judge Dave Aughinbaugh, Nick Menges, Benjamin Carney, Aaron Tesler; Judge Nick Agan, Sara Agan, Darin Elm, Jack Dillman, Karim "The Dream" Ayyad, Jason Mycol Allen; Judge Ross Miller: Alex Rangel, James Chodes, Travis Samonas, Kyle Fruehe, Sarah Hansen, Robert Abrahamian; Judge Spencer Ellsworth, Derrick Record, Colton Sybouts, Mike Sutcliffe, Kim Sutcliffe; Judge David Gallico, Joseph Bardsley, Daryl Phillips, Laurence Tilley

ehold! Once again it is time for the unrelenting gaze of the Phlogistonic Eye to peer across the multiverse. It perceives all, knows all! Staring into the very hearts of mortals to uncover that which drives them to create. Observing the daily lives of these tiny wretches as they gather for comfort in a cold, uncaring universe. The Eye looks upon you. Dare you look back? Author Stephen Newton meets the Eye's stare and has this to say about DCC #105 By Mitra's Bones, Meet Thy Doom!

I was incredibly excited when presented with the opportunity to expand upon the world of Jennell Jaquays' *Dark Tower* universe. *Dark Tower* is truly epic in scope and introduces us to the denizens of Mitra's Fist, the journey of Mitra from mortal to god, the rise of the towers, the soul gems, and dozens of NPCs all with intriguing backstories. With so much possible material to expand upon, the question became: where to focus?

I re-read the original *Dark Tower* paying attention to the history, NPCs, and themes within the adventure. There were two story elements that stood as exciting areas to expand the mythos. The first regarded the degenerate NPC Avvakris and his three children (Aphris, Avvala, and Avvaar); all had interesting backstories, but the mother is only mentioned once as "his late wife" and it is suggested that Aphis' real father is a minion of Set. Building upon that missing character and the rumor of Aphis' true father seemed like a great adventure seed. But where to place her?

The second story element that intrigued me: according to the history of Dark Tower, the mortal Mitra slays Set in *demon* form. It made me think: through this actions, did Mitra inadvertently pave the way for Set to evolve from mere demon to powerful deity?

I created a timeline based on the events described in the history section of Dark Tower, diagramming major milestones: the of death of Mitra, when his followers started erecting temples in his name, the creation of the "White Tower", and other significant events. I found it interesting that Set created the eponymous dark tower directly opposite Mitra's white tower. Thus, the concept that Set—for reasons only known to gods—would feel compelled to set up "opposing" temples of near equal strength next to the temples created in Mitra's name felt like a core tenet of the Dark *Tower* vibe.

Those two elements, along with the motif of opposites, became the skeleton of my adventure. I asked myself: if Av-

Author Stephen Newton

vakris' wife (whom I named "Avvani"), a purported consort of a Minion of Set, was not in Mitra's Fist, then where would she be? I posited that if Mitra's followers were creating multiple temples in his name, then Set would be creating opposing temples nearby and that's where Avvani must have been during the fall of Mitra's Fist.

As a fan of history, I am familiar with stories of religions incorporating holy relics such as the bones of saints into their churches as a means of attracting followers and providing blessings. (In fact, in the original *Dark Tower* adventure, Mitra's hip bone is located in a reliquary in area 1-40!) I was also inspired by other religious lore of statues which have been reported to perform miracles. Using these legends as inspiration, I wrote that Mitra's physical teeth were housed as relics in a new temple dedicated in his name. (Note: in my adventure, the statue of Mitra itself with Mitra's Jawbone was inspired by the "Chatterbox" cenobite from Clive Barker's, *Hellraiser*.) The original *Dark Tower* also describes a "gorgeous, blonde woman" —elsewhere described as a beautiful maiden—who kisses the forehead of a character when bestowing the soul gem the Heart of Law (see Dark Tower area 1-42). I felt this "angel" would be a significant part of the fledgling Mitraic religion and incorporated her statue as the one that would reportedly able to perform miracles. The "Field of Leonids" (area 5-3) was inspired by the "tuning fork portal" from the movie *Phantasm*. Avvani and her brother becoming lovers after centuries and creating a "false temple" atop the real temple of Mitra just felt like a *Dark Tower*-y thing to do.

Geb, the father of Snakes, was written after seeing Aaron Kreader's draft of the cover art for the adventure! And Mahna, the main antagonist of Set's temple, was an opportunity to introduce a "Runt of Set" (as opposed to a Chosen or Lesser Son), providing backstory as to how Avvani came to mother the reptilian Aphis.

My ultimate goal, of course, was to create a fun and exciting adventure that captured the *Dark Tower* vibe of rich backstory, open-ended maps, interesting NPCs, and extending the battle of Mitra vs. Set. I sincerely hope the adventure is fun for players who no experience with *Dark Tower*, but provides additional joy for folks familiar with the original material.

The Phlogistonic Eye often stares into the strange corners of the multiverse, witnessing things undreamt of by god and mortal. It watches the struggle between Set and Mitra with great interest and is pleased to see the battle continue in the pages of this adventure. Look for the next withering gaze of the Phlogistonic Eye in future DCC RPG publications coming to a marketplace near you!

IN MEMORIAM: JENNELL JAQUAYS

Shortly before publishing this adventure, it was announced that Jennell Jaquays had passed away. To say that Jennell was an icon in this industry would be an understatement. Her classic adventures *Caverns of Thracia* and *Dark Tower* are some of the most beloved modules of all time, with *Dark Tower* actually included in Dungeon Magazine's *30 Greatest D&D Adventures of All Time* article. Jennell was equally talented as an artist, with her illustrations appearing in her own adventures, on the covers of RPG magazines such as *Dragon*, and Jennell even made a successful transition to working on computer games.

Aside from a few occasional likes or comments on social media posts, I never had the privilege of working with Jennell. And while we never met in person, Jennell's works have nonetheless had a major influence on how I think about NPCs and adventure design. Her innovative, open-ended maps and memorable NPCs with rich backstories and motivations set the gold standard for me as to what a well-designed adventure could achieve. The continued demand and popularity of her adventures 40-plus years after their initial publication is proof of what an enormous talent Jennell was. By creating such enduring stories and artwork, she leaves behind for us a gift of imagination which will continue to inspire designers for many more years to come. You need to look no further than the adventure you are currently holding in your hands: it literally would not exist without her.

This week while reading all the posts and memories how others were impacted by Jennell's writing and art, it is clear to me that I am not alone in how profoundly I was touched by her creations. And while she will be missed by many, I'm positive that Jennell's legacy will continue to flourish in the decades to come as a new generation of gamers becomes familiar with her works through the *Original Adventures Reincarnated* line and other reprints. Godspeed, Jennell, you will be remembered.

Stephen Newton – Jan 2024

We're with the band